21st Century Disasters

Hawaii Volcano of 2018

by Shannon Berg

FOCUS READERS

BEACON

www.focusreaders.com

Focus Readers is distributed by North Star Editions:
sales@northstareditions.com | 888-417-0195

Produced for Focus Readers by Red Line Editorial.

Photographs ©: USGS Hawaiian Volcano Observatory/US Geological Survey, cover, 1, 4, 6, 10, 13, 24, 27; Red Line Editorial, 8; HQPhotos/E+/Getty Images, 15; US Geological Survey/Anadolu Agency/Getty Images, 16–17; US Geological Survey/Getty Images News/Getty Images, 18; G. E. Ulrich/US Geological Survey, 21, 29; Josh Cornish/Shutterstock Images, 23

Library of Congress Cataloging-in-Publication Data
Names: Berg, Shannon, author.
Title: Hawaii volcano of 2018 / by Shannon Berg.
Description: Lake Elmo, MN : Focus Readers, [2020] | Series: 21st century disasters | Audience: Grade 4 to 6. | Includes index.
Identifiers: LCCN 2019002272 (print) | LCCN 2019010691 (ebook) | ISBN 9781641859462 (PDF) | ISBN 9781641858779 (ebook) | ISBN 9781641857390 (hardcover) | ISBN 9781641858083 (pbk.)
Subjects: LCSH: Kilauea Volcano (Hawaii)--Eruption, 2018. | Kilauea Volcano (Hawaii)--Juvenile literature. | Volcanoes--Hawaii--Juvenile literature. | Volcanic eruptions--Juvenile literature.
Classification: LCC QE523.K5 (ebook) | LCC QE523.K5 B47 2020 (print) | DDC 363.34/95099691--dc23
LC record available at https://lccn.loc.gov/2019002272

Printed in the United States of America
Mankato, MN
May, 2019

About the Author

Shannon Berg is a young adult novelist, short story and nonfiction author, and poet. Shannon lives in Minnesota with her husband, two children, dog, and cat. Most of her spare time is spent working her way through the stack of books waiting to be read on her nightstand.

Table of Contents

Chapter 1

Eruption!

On May 3, 2018, scientists sounded an alarm. It warned people that a volcano was going to **erupt**. The volcano's name is Kilauea. It is on the Big Island of Hawaii.

A huge cloud of smoke and ash rises from Kilauea in May 2018.

A river of lava flows from Kilauea and covers the land around it.

Kilauea is an active volcano. That means it can still erupt. Kilauea is the most active volcano in the world. Most of its eruptions are small. But the one in 2018 was much bigger. **Lava** poured out of the volcano.

Many people live near Kilauea. The lava flowed toward their homes. They had to **evacuate**. Maddy Welch was one of them. Maddy left her home. She took her pets with her. She went somewhere safe. Then she waited for the eruption to end.

Volcanoes erupt for more than just one day. In fact, they can erupt for weeks, months, or even years.

KILAUEA ERUPTION TIMELINE

May 2
Cracks open in the ground near Kilauea.

May 3
More cracks form, and lava begins flowing from the volcano.

May 9
The volcano begins sending rocks and ash thousands of feet into the air.

May 19
The river of lava reaches the ocean.

June 24
As eruptions continue, the clouds of ash and steam begin getting smaller.

August 3
Kilauea's eruptions finally start to slow.

Kilauea erupted from May until August. It spewed rocks and ash into the air. Some went as high as 30,000 feet (9,000 m).

The volcano kept erupting. A river of lava reached all the way to the ocean. It swallowed roads and houses along the way.

Finally, in early August, the eruptions slowed down. By then, lava had destroyed more than 700 houses.

Did You Know?

The state of Hawaii is made up of several islands. Volcanoes began forming them millions of years ago.

Chapter 2

Understanding Volcanoes

A volcano is a vent, or opening, in Earth's **crust**. The crust is made of pieces called plates. The plates float on a layer of melted rock. Vents often form at places where these plates join.

Volcanoes send up hot, melted rock from deep beneath Earth's surface.

Magma collects in a space beneath the vent. This space is called a chamber.

When a volcano erupts, magma moves up through the chamber. Sometimes volcanoes erupt because of earthquakes. Earthquakes shake the ground.

Did You Know?

Volcanoes can be found on every continent, including Antarctica. But most of the world's volcanoes are underwater.

Melted rock is called magma when it is beneath Earth's crust. Above ground, it is called lava.

They send magma up through the vent.

Other times, volcanoes erupt because of gases. The gases mix together in the chamber. They build up pressure. When this force grows strong enough, magma shoots up out of the vent.

When magma goes above Earth's crust, it is called lava. Sometimes lava pours out over the ground. Other times, it shoots up into the air. Volcanoes can also send out blasts of rock and ash.

Lava hardens as it cools. Over time, the lava piles up. It builds the volcano. Volcanoes can have several

Did You Know?

Sometimes a volcano's top collapses. It forms a hole known as a caldera.

Kilauea has a large crater at its top. This round hole formed when part of the volcano collapsed.

shapes. Some form tall cones. Others look like a hill of rock. Shield volcanoes are wide and round. Their sides have gentle slopes. Kilauea is a shield volcano.

BE PREPARED

Volcanoes

Lava destroys everything in its path. No one can stop lava or hold it back. People must get out of the way. People who live near volcanoes must be ready to leave quickly. They should have an evacuation plan. They should also prepare disaster kits.

A disaster kit holds supplies people might need after a volcano. It includes food and water. It should have towels and dust masks. These things keep people from breathing the ash in the air. A radio provides news about the volcano. First aid supplies help if people get hurt.

Lava rushes down a street in Hawaii.

Chapter 3

Survivor Stories

When Kilauea began erupting, many people had to evacuate. One was Amber Makuakane Kane. She worked as a teacher. Lava began flowing toward the town where she lived.

Dark, hardened lava covers the ground near Pahoa, Hawaii.

Amber and her two children drove to safety. But lava destroyed their house. They lost everything they owned.

Many people went to stay in **shelters**. Some people lived in the shelters for months. They didn't know if their homes would still be there when they returned.

Did You Know?

Some lava flowed into a lake. The lava's heat caused the water to boil away.

Kilauea has erupted many times in the past. This photo shows a 1983 eruption.

Mary Dressler knew how the people at the shelters felt. Mary had lost her home when Kilauea erupted years earlier. Lava burned through her whole town in 1990.

Mary wanted to help **victims** of the 2018 eruption. Other people joined her. Some people donated clothes. Others gave out food and water.

Harry Kim was the mayor of the Big Island. He lost a house to the volcano. Kim talked to other people who had lost homes. He worked to find them new places to live.

Many people chose to stay and rebuild. Living near a volcano is dangerous. But volcanoes bring good things, too. The soil near

Ferns can begin growing very soon after lava hardens.

volcanoes is good for growing plants. That is one reason Hawaii is so green.

Chapter 4

Changed Forever

When a volcano erupts, it changes the shape of the land around it. Sometimes, lava piles up and makes mountains grow. Other times, the blasts break up parts of the volcano.

When lava reaches the sea, the water cools it and sends up huge clouds of steam.

In 2018, Kilauea's **peak** fell in. The eruption also created new beaches. Lava flowed down near the ocean. Black sand beaches formed where the lava touched the water.

Scientists study volcanoes to see if they are active. They **monitor** pressure in the gases and

Did You Know?

By July 13, the lava flowing from Kilauea into the ocean formed a small new island.

A scientist checks a crack in the ground for changes in temperature.

earthquakes in the ground. Then they warn people if an eruption is coming. Scientists can even make maps of where lava will flow. They work to help people stay safe.

FOCUS ON

Hawaii Volcano of 2018

Write your answers on a separate piece of paper.

1. Write a sentence summarizing Chapter 3.
2. Would you want to live near a volcano? Why or why not?
3. What is the name for magma that has moved above Earth's surface?
   - **A.** ash
   - **B.** vent
   - **C.** lava
4. Why can mapping where lava flows help protect people after an eruption?
   - **A.** Scientists can warn people in places where the lava will go.
   - **B.** People can spray water on the lava to slow it down.
   - **C.** Workers can build fences to stop the lava.

5. What does **pressure** mean in this book?

They build up ***pressure****. When this force grows strong enough, magma shoots up out of the vent.*

- **A.** stress or tension
- **B.** lots of money
- **C.** loud noises

6. What does **donated** mean in this book?

Some people ***donated*** *clothes. Others gave out food and water.*

- **A.** threw something away
- **B.** hid something to keep it safe
- **C.** gave something away to help others

Answer key on page 32.

Glossary

crust
Earth's hard outer layer.

erupt
To send lava, hot ashes, and steam out of the ground, sometimes high into the air.

evacuate
To leave a place of danger.

lava
Hot, melted rock that is released by a volcano onto Earth's surface.

magma
Hot, melted rock under Earth's surface.

monitor
To keep track of something over time.

peak
The top of a mountain.

shelters
Places, especially temporary ones, where people can stay when they have to leave their homes.

victims
People who have been harmed by an event or accident.

To Learn More

BOOKS

Farndon, John. *Extreme Volcanoes.* Minneapolis: Hungry Tomato, 2018.

Mattern, Joanne. *Hawai‘i.* New York: Children's Press, 2018.

Reynolds, Shaye. *Volcanoes.* New York: PowerKids Press, 2017.

NOTE TO EDUCATORS

Visit **www.focusreaders.com** to find lesson plans, activities, links, and other resources related to this title.

Index

Answer Key: 1. Answers will vary; **2.** Answers will vary; **3.** C; **4.** A; **5.** A; **6.** C